Lucas

GRAPHIC DINOSAURS

STEGOSAURUS

THE PLATED DINOSAUR

ILLUSTRATED BY JAMES FIELD

PowerKiDS
press.

New York

Published in 2009 by The Rosen Publishing Group, Inc.
29 East 21st Street, New York 10010

Designed and produced by
David West Books

Designed and written by Gary Jeffrey
Editor: Ronne Randall
Consultant: Steve Parker, Senior Scientific Fellow, Zoological Society of London
Photographic credits: 5t, Postdlf, wikipedia project; 5r, AndonicO, en.wikipedia.org: 5b, Lee R. Berger; 30 (main), hibino, en.wikipedia.org, 30 (inset) Chris Gladis, en.wikipedia.org.

Library of Congress Cataloging-in-Publication Data

Jeffrey, Gary.
Stegosaurus : the plated dinosaur / Gary Jeffrey.
p.cm. — (Graphic dinosaurs)
Includes index.
ISBN 978-1-4358-2503-1 (library binding)
ISBN 978-1-4042-7713-7 (pbk.)
ISBN 978-1-4042-7717-5 (6-pack)
1. Stegosaurus—Juvenile literature. I. Title.
QE862.O65J44 2009
567.915'3—dc22

2007050587

Manufactured in China

CONTENTS

 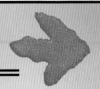

WHAT IS A STEGOSAURUS?

STEGOSAURUS MEANS "ROOF LIZARD"

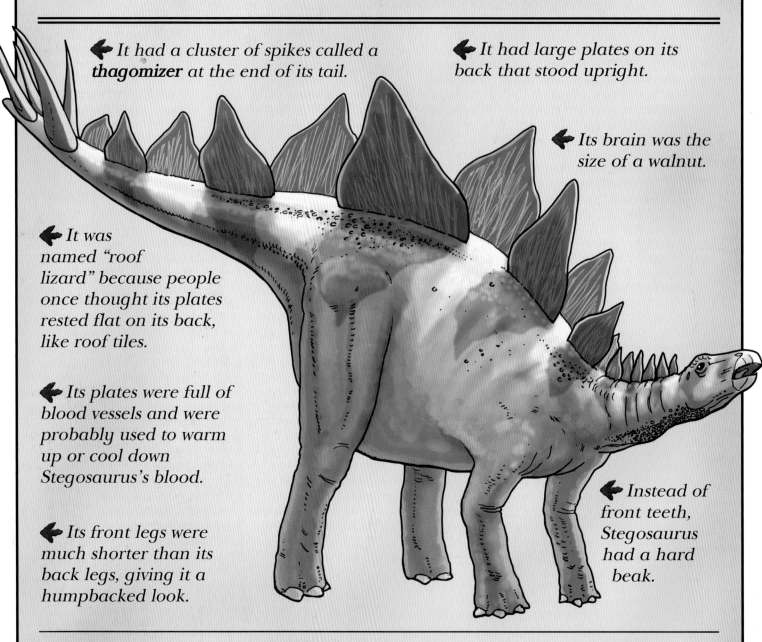

It had a cluster of spikes called a **thagomizer** at the end of its tail.

It had large plates on its back that stood upright.

Its brain was the size of a walnut.

It was named "roof lizard" because people once thought its plates rested flat on its back, like roof tiles.

Its plates were full of blood vessels and were probably used to warm up or cool down Stegosaurus's blood.

Its front legs were much shorter than its back legs, giving it a humpbacked look.

Instead of front teeth, Stegosaurus had a hard beak.

STEGOSAURUS LIVED AROUND 160 MILLION TO 145 MILLION YEARS AGO, DURING THE JURASSIC PERIOD. FOSSILS OF ITS SKELETON HAVE BEEN FOUND IN NORTH AMERICA AND PORTUGAL (SEE PAGE 30).

Adult Stegosauruses measured up to 30 feet (9 m) long, and 14 feet (4 m) high at the top of the tallest back plate. They weighed 5.5 tons (4,989 kg).

SMALL-BRAINED

A plaster cast was made of the inside of a Stegosaurus brain case. It was the size of a walnut, making it the smallest brain (in relation to body size) of any dinosaur. A larger cluster of nerves at the base of Stegosaurus's spine may have acted like a second brain, helping it move quickly when attacked. Stegosaurus was as smart as it needed to be to **survive**.

A walnut at actual size.

PIECES OF A PUZZLE

The purpose of Stegosaurus's 17 plates is still a mystery. **Paleontologists** generally agree that they were too thin to have been used for armor. Being full of blood vessels, they could have been made to blush red and warn off approaching attackers. The strong outline of the plates would also have helped Stegosauruses spot their own kind among other dinosaurs.

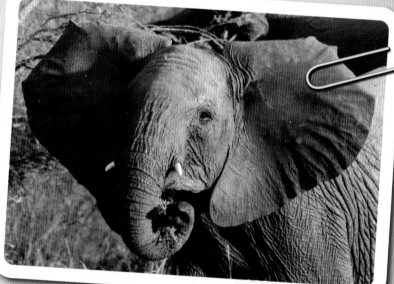

HEAT EXCHANGERS?

Just as African elephants' large ears help to cool their blood, Stegosaurus's back plates may have controlled its body temperature.

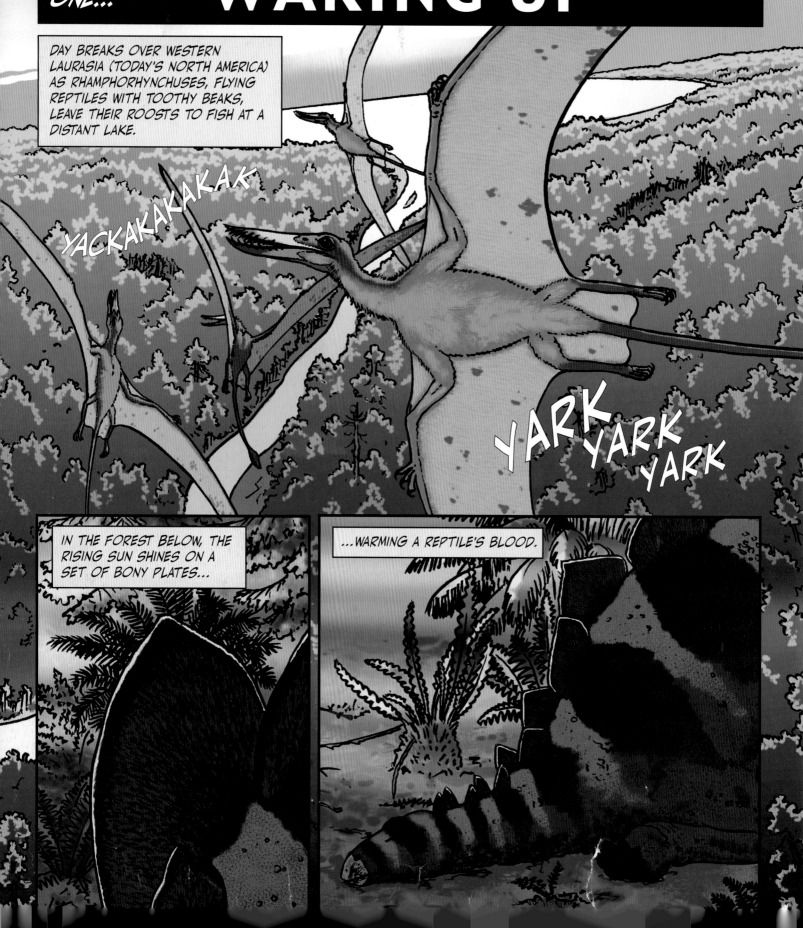

PART ONE... WAKING UP

DAY BREAKS OVER WESTERN LAURASIA (TODAY'S NORTH AMERICA) AS RHAMPHORHYNCHUSES, FLYING REPTILES WITH TOOTHY BEAKS, LEAVE THEIR ROOSTS TO FISH AT A DISTANT LAKE.

YACKAKAKAKAK

YARK YARK YARK

IN THE FOREST BELOW, THE RISING SUN SHINES ON A SET OF BONY PLATES...

...WARMING A REPTILE'S BLOOD.

SHE YAWNS.

GWAAAAARGH

THE NOISE STARTLES A MAMMAL, CALLED A FRUITAFOSSOR, WHO IS FEASTING ON SWARMING TERMITES.

SQUEEEEE

LIFTING HER HEAVY FRAME, THE **JUVENILE** STEGOSAURUS CALLS OUT TO THE ADULTS IN HER GROUP.

BWOAAAAAARK!

ALTHOUGH JUST THREE YEARS OLD, SHE IS ALREADY OVER 6 FEET (2 M) LONG. HER CALL IS A DEEP BELLOW THAT SAYS "GET UP! IT IS TIME TO FEED!"

SQUEEEEE SQUEEEE

IT IS THE DRY SEASON. THE GROUP FOLLOWS A BULL, OR MALE, TO FEED IN THE FORESTS THAT GROW ALONG A RIVER.

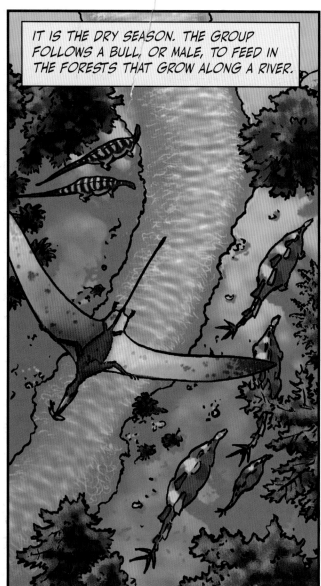

HERE, WHERE THE PLANTS HAVE STAYED LUSH, THEY BREAKFAST ON FIR LEAVES, FERNS, AND GIANT CYCADS.

RRRRRIIIIPPPP

THESE RIVER FORESTS ARE HOME TO ALL KINDS OF DINOSAURS. SMALL OTHNIELIAS RUSH IN TO PICK OVER THE DEBRIS LEFT IN THE STEGOSAURUSES' TRAIL.

DELLLWHIP

GWEEEP

WHWILELLLWHIP

THE JUVENILE STEGOSAURUS SNIFFS AT A CYCAD. IT IS VERY TEMPTING, BUT JUST OUT OF REACH.

SNUFFFLE SNIFF

WANTING A CHANGE FROM THE BORING, LOW-GROWING FERNS, SHE REARS UP.

DELLWHUP

SHE IS UNAWARE...

...THAT SHE IS BEING WATCHED.

THE WATCHER APPEARS. IT IS A CERATOSAURUS, A FIERCE MEAT EATER. HIS JAWS ARE STRONG ENOUGH TO CAUSE A SERIOUS WOUND.

GRRRAAAGH

THE OTHNIELIAS PANIC.

GLAAAARRRKK

THE STEGOSAURUS CRIES OUT IN ALARM...

GWEEEEEEEE

...BUT TODAY SHE IS NOT THE PREY.

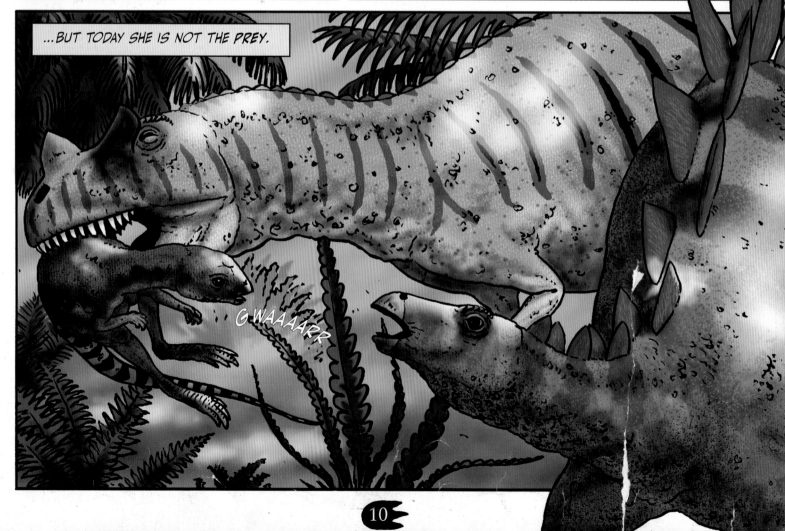

GWAAAARR

WARNED BY THE YOUNG ONE'S CRIES, THE ADULTS GATHER.

ALTHOUGH NOT YET AN ADULT, THE CERATOSAURUS IS SEEN AS A SERIOUS THREAT BY THE ADULT STEGOSAURUSES.

THE SPIKY WALL THEY PUT UP ALARMS THE PREDATOR.

THE CERATOSAURUS STALKS OFF TO EAT HIS PRIZE IN PEACE.

THE FOREST HAS BECOME QUIET AGAIN. WHILE THE ADULTS CONTINUE FEEDING, THE JUVENILE STEGOSAURUS PRACTICES SWINGING HER TAIL SPIKES.

INSPIRED BY THE ADULTS' EARLIER DISPLAY, SHE FLEXES HER TAIL MUSCLES...

...WHICH ARE ALREADY...

BOK!

...QUITE STRONG.

CRRRACCK!

PART TWO... THE WATERING HOLE

IN THE HEAT OF THE DAY, THE STEGOSAURUSES HAVE MADE THEIR WAY TO THE LAKE.

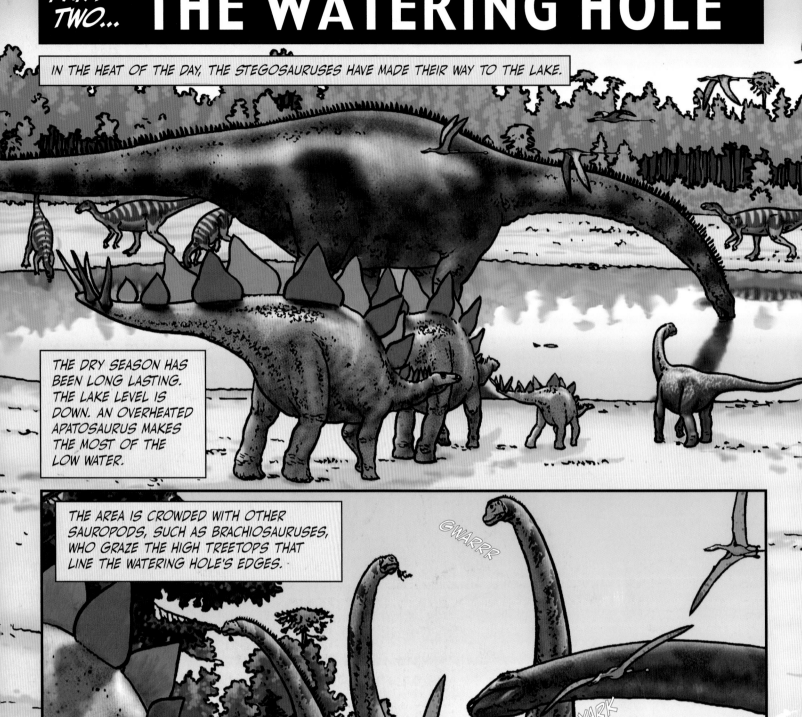

THE DRY SEASON HAS BEEN LONG LASTING. THE LAKE LEVEL IS DOWN. AN OVERHEATED APATOSAURUS MAKES THE MOST OF THE LOW WATER.

THE AREA IS CROWDED WITH OTHER SAUROPODS, SUCH AS BRACHIOSAURUSES, WHO GRAZE THE HIGH TREETOPS THAT LINE THE WATERING HOLE'S EDGES.

A JUVENILE CAMARASAURUS BLOCKS THE WAY TO THE WATER.

THE JUVENILE STEGOSAURUS CHALLENGES THE YOUNG SAUROPOD. "MOVE BACK!" SHE GROWLS.

GWAAAAARRRK!

THE CAMARASAURUS IS FRIGHTENED BY THE SPIKY NEWCOMER AND TAKES OFF...

GWEEEEEEEK

...BACK TO ITS PARENT.

GWEEEEK GWEEEK

THE ADULT CAMARASAURUS RESPONDS TO THE THREAT BY RAISING A BIG CLAWED FOOT...

BROOAARRGH

...AND MOVING IN.

RRRAAAGH

BOOM

THE JUVENILE IS ABOUT TO BE TRAMPLED.

GWEEEP!

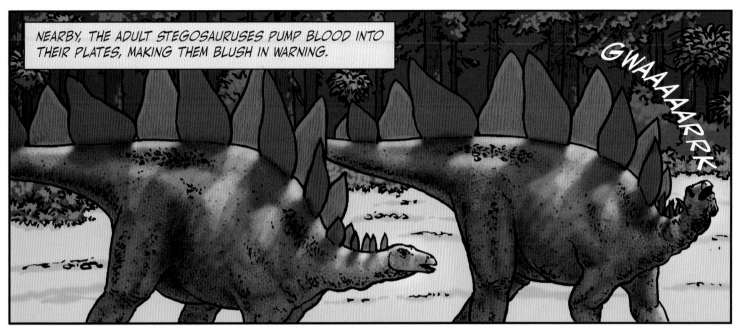

NEARBY, THE ADULT STEGOSAURUSES PUMP BLOOD INTO THEIR PLATES, MAKING THEM BLUSH IN WARNING.

GWAAAARRK

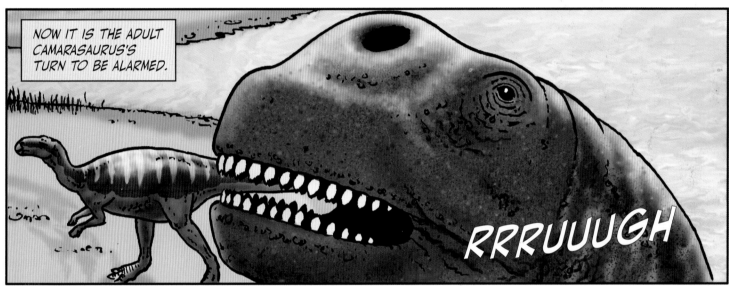

NOW IT IS THE ADULT CAMARASAURUS'S TURN TO BE ALARMED.

RRRUUUGH

THE CAMARASAURUS BACKS AWAY AS THE TERRIFIED JUVENILE STEGOSAURUS TAKES **REFUGE** IN THE FOREST.

BWAAAARUUUUUGH

GWEEEEEEEEEE

PART THREE... **TRAPPED**

THE STEGOSAURUS HAS COME TO REST BY A STREAM AND SOMETHING HAS CAUGHT HER ATTENTION.

SHE SEES FOOTPRINTS AND A BROKEN EGG.

BWOOOAAAAR

SNUFFLE SNUFFLE

THERE ARE MORE. SHE FOLLOWS THE TRAIL.

THE SOURCE OF THE BROKEN EGGS BECOMES CLEAR.

CRACKLE CRACKLE

AN ORNITHOLESTES IS ATTACKING AN ABANDONED CAMPTOSAURUS'S NEST.

BZZZZZZZZZZ

GLUMMMMNGH

HER ATTENTION IS ON THE NEST ROBBER, SO THE STEGOSAURUS FAILS TO NOTICE THAT SOMETHING HAS SLIPPED INTO THE WATER BEHIND HER...

GWOOOOP

...AND IS MOVING TOWARD HER.

GWEEEP

THE CERATOSAURUS LEAPS FROM THE STREAM...

BORAAAAAAGH!

...BUT, YET AGAIN, THE STEGOSAURUS...

GWEEEEEEEEE

...IS NOT THE PREY.

GNAARRRF

GWAAAARRRR

20

FEARING ATTACK, THE JUVENILE TURNS TO LEAVE THE FOREST...

...BUT THE WAY AHEAD IS BLOCKED...

...BY AN ALLOSAURUS!

GWRRRRRRRRR

THIS KING OF THE MEAT EATERS HAS COME TO SATISFY HIS THIRST. HE HAS BEEN FEEDING ON A CAMPTOSAURUS WHO WANDERED ACROSS HIS PATH.

LOOKING BEYOND THE ALLOSAURUS, THE STEGOSAURUS CAN SEE HER GROUP MOVING AWAY.

SLUUUURRP SLUUURRP

SHE TURNS TO CHECK ON THE CERATOSAURUS AND INTERRUPTS HIS MEAL. HE DROPS THE ORNITHOLESTES AND COMES AFTER HER.

BOOOUWAAAGH

HOLDING HER GROUND, SHE WIGGLES HER TAIL SPIKES AT HER ATTACKER...

...BUT THE CERATOSAURUS KEEPS COMING.

GRRRAAAAGH

SHE HAS NO CHOICE. SHE MUST RUN PAST THE ALLOSAURUS.

AS THE ALLOSAURUS DRINKS, SHE MOVES...

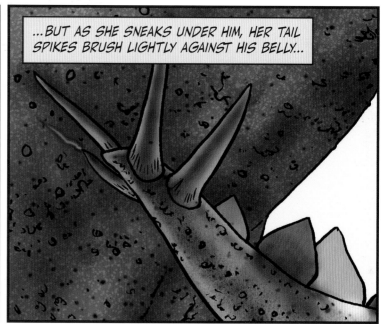

...BUT AS SHE SNEAKS UNDER HIM, HER TAIL SPIKES BRUSH LIGHTLY AGAINST HIS BELLY...

...LETTING HIM KNOW SHE'S THERE.

GRRRAAGH

THE ALLOSAURUS CHASES HER.

GRRAAA

DOUFFF

HE IS EXCITED BY THE PROMISE OF MORE FRESH MEAT.

SPLOSH!

GRRRRRRRRRRRRRRRR

THE ALLOSAURUS IS WEIGHED DOWN BY HIS RECENT MEAL.

BWAARK

THE STEGOSAURUS REACHES THE SAFETY OF HER GROUP.

GRRRRRRRRRRRRRRRR

THE BULL STEGOSAURUS HOLDS HIS GROUND. THE PREDATOR IS TOO CLOSE TO OUTRUN NOW.

BWAARK

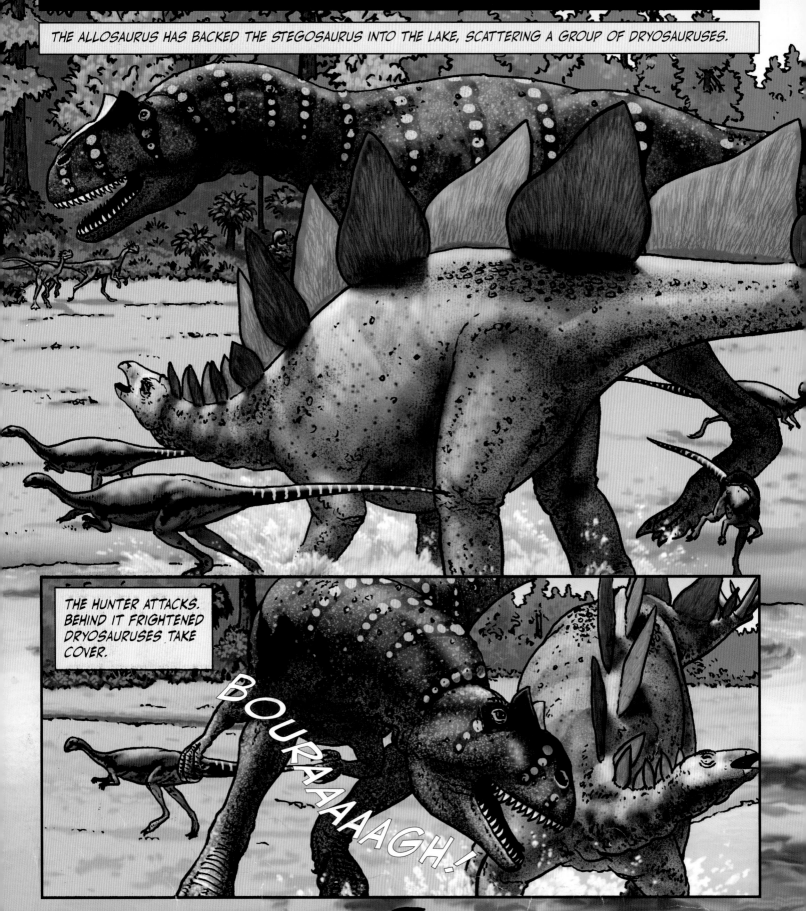

PART FOUR... DEATH MATCH

THE ALLOSAURUS HAS BACKED THE STEGOSAURUS INTO THE LAKE, SCATTERING A GROUP OF DRYOSAURUSES.

THE HUNTER ATTACKS. BEHIND IT FRIGHTENED DRYOSAURUSES TAKE COVER.

BOURAAAAAGH!

SPINNING ON HIS HIND LEGS, THE STEGOSAURUS DESPERATELY TWISTS AWAY...

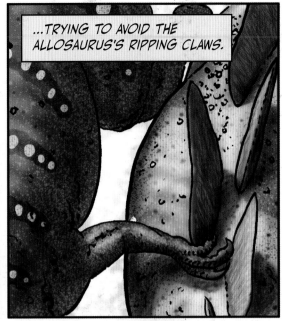

...TRYING TO AVOID THE ALLOSAURUS'S RIPPING CLAWS.

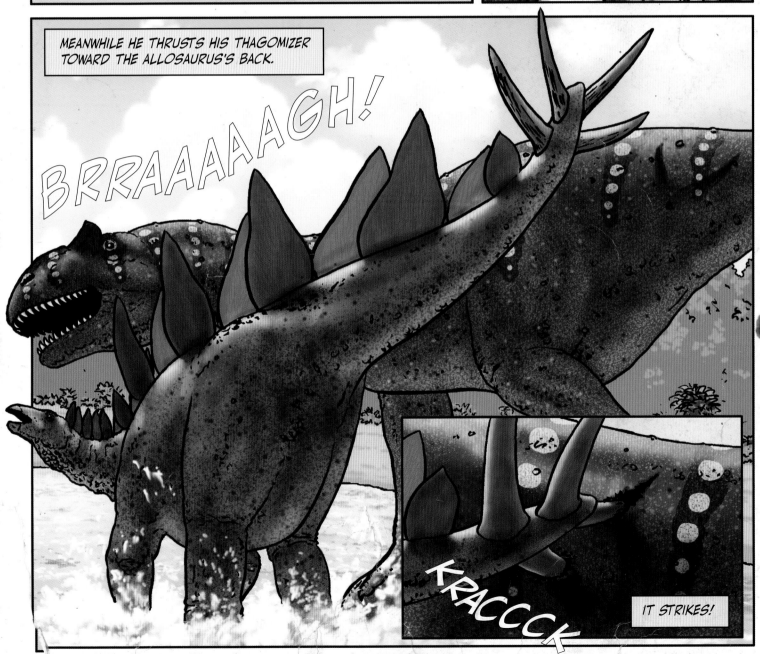

MEANWHILE HE THRUSTS HIS THAGOMIZER TOWARD THE ALLOSAURUS'S BACK.

BRRAAAAAGH!

KRACCCK

IT STRIKES!

AAAAAAARRRRGGGG

THE BLOW TEARS INTO THE MEAT EATER'S FLESH AND CAUSES MASSIVE BLEEDING.

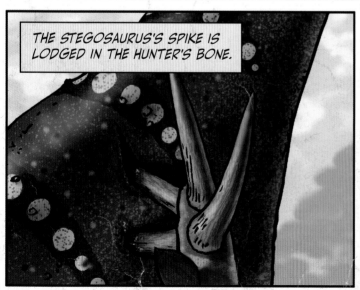

THE STEGOSAURUS'S SPIKE IS LODGED IN THE HUNTER'S BONE.

BUT IT BREAKS OFF.

KRAK!

THE GROUP MOVES AWAY, LEAVING THE ALLOSAURUS TO ITS FATE.

GRRRRAAAAAAAAGH

GWEEEP

THE BULL HAS LOST PART OF A TAIL SPIKE, BUT HE WILL LIVE TO FIGHT ANOTHER DAY...

...UNLIKE THE ALLOSAURUS.

AS THE STEGOSAURUSES HEAD TOWARD THE FOREST, THE SKY DARKENS. THE WET-SEASON RAINS ARE COMING.

GWAAAARF!

THE LITTLE STEGOSAUR WILL SLEEP WELL TONIGHT.

FOSSIL EVIDENCE

WE CAN GET A GOOD IDEA OF WHAT DINOSAURS MAY HAVE LOOKED LIKE FROM THEIR FOSSILS. FOSSILS ARE FORMED WHEN THE HARD PARTS OF AN ANIMAL OR PLANT BECOME BURIED AND THEN TURN TO ROCK OVER MILLIONS OF YEARS.

Paleontologists think that the Stegosaurus's thagomizer (inset below) might have been used as a defensive weapon. In 2005, a Stegosaurus neck plate was shown to have bite marks that matched the teeth pattern of an Allosaurus. An Allosaurus backbone had a hole in which a Stegosaurus thagomizer fitted perfectly. Over the years, many of the fossil thagomizers that have been dug up have had broken tips. This suggests that Stegosauruses and Allosauruses did indeed fight with each other, as shown in so many reconstructions (below).

DINOSAUR GALLERY

ALL THESE DINOSAURS APPEAR IN THE STORY.

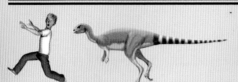 

Othnielia
"For Othniel"
Length: 5 ft (1.5 m)
A small, birdlike dinosaur named after famed fossil hunter Othniel Charles Marsh.

Ornitholestes
"Bird robber"
Length: 6 ft (2 m)
A small, active meat eater with long forearms, which may have eaten eggs.

Dryosaurus
"Oak lizard"
Length: 10–13 ft (3–4 m)
A small to medium-sized plant eater with unusual oak-leaf-shaped teeth.

Camptosaurus
"Bent lizard"
Length: 26 ft (8 m)
A heavy-set plant eater that likely walked on four legs, but could raise itself up on two legs to reach food.

Ceratosaurus
"Horned lizard"
Length: 20–26 ft (6–8 m)
A large meat eater with a big nose horn and bony crests in front of its eyes. It also had a thick tail like a crocodile's and may have been a good swimmer.

Allosaurus
"Different lizard"
Length: 30–42 ft (8.5–13 m)
A large meat eater with strong front claws. It was at the top of the late Jurassic food chain.

Camarasaurus
"Chambered lizard"
Length: 60 ft (18 m)
A giant, strongly-built plant eater that had nostrils in front of and above its eyes.

GLOSSARY

cycads (SY-kudz) Fernlike evergreen plants that have short, fat trunks.

fossils (FAH-sulz) The remains of living things that have turned to rock.

Jurassic period (ju-RA-sik PIR-ee-ud) The time between 200 million and 145 million years ago.

juvenile (JOO-veh-ny-uhl) Not fully grown.

paleontologists (pay-lee-on-TO-luh-jists) Scientists who study fossils.

prey (PRAY) Animals that are hunted for food by another animal.

refuge (REH-fyooj) Protection.

survive (sur-VYV) To stay alive.

thagomizer (THAG-oh-my-zer) A Stegosaurus's tail spikes.

INDEX

Web Sites

Due to the changing nature of Internet links, the Rosen Publishing Group, Inc., has developed an online list of Web sites related to the subject of this book. This site is updated regularly. Please use this link to access the list:

www.powerkidslinks.com/gdino/stego/